THE GREAT GRANNY DUST-UP

by

ANDREW MATTHEWS

Illustrated by Annie Horwood

HAMISH HAMILTON
LONDON

For Rob, Kate, Carys, Jessica and Toby

HAMISH HAMILTON LTD

Published by the Penguin Group
27 Wrights Lane, London w8 5tz, England
Penguin Books USA Inc., 375 Hudson Street, New York, New York 10014, USA
Penguin Books Australia Ltd, Ringwood, Victoria, Australia
Penguin Books Canada Ltd, 10 Alcorn Avenue, Toronto, Ontario, Canada m4v 3b2
Penguin Books (NZ) Ltd, 182–190 Wairau Road, Auckland 10, New Zealand

Penguin Books Ltd, Registered Offices: Harmondsworth, Middlesex, England

First published in Great Britain 1992 by Hamish Hamilton Ltd

Text copyright © 1992 by Andrew Matthews
Illustrations copyright © 1992 by Annie Horwood

1 3 5 7 9 10 8 6 4 2

British Library Cataloguing in Publication Data
CIP data for this book is available from the British Library

ISBN 0-241-13156-1

Set in 15pt Baskerville by Rowland Phototypesetting Ltd
Bury St Edmunds, Suffolk
Printed in Great Britain by BPCC Hazells Ltd
Member of BPCC Ltd

Duelling Grannies

Chapter 1

WHEN THE SHEPPARDS returned from their summer holiday, they usually had one of the grannies to stay for a week. The grannies took it in turns and they were very particular about whose turn it was. Dad said they probably made a note in their diaries. Joan said they probably counted the notches on their broomsticks, and got told off. This year, it was to be Granny Crump's turn.

The surprise phone call came two days after the family ended their holiday on the Norfolk Broads. It came

in the middle of dinner. Dinner was
stuffed marrow and Alice had cooked
it. As soon as the phone rang, Mum,
Dad and Robert looked up eagerly,
saying, "I'll get it!" but Mum was first
to her feet. She practically sprinted out
of the dining room.

Alice peered suspiciously at Dad and
Robert. They were moving bits of
stuffed marrow about on their plates,
but none of the bits actually ended up

in their mouths. The only person who was eating was Joan. She was eating sausages and chips, covered with so much tomato sauce that her plate looked like an operation. She seethed happily to the music in the headphones of her personal stereo.

"Why does Joan never eat the same food as the rest of us?" Robert asked resentfully.

"Because she makes a loud noise that goes on for a very long time if we try and make her," Dad explained. "Besides, she's going through her junk-food phase. It makes young children very touchy."

Alice suddenly narrowed her eyes.

"You don't like my stuffed marrow, do you?" she asked her father and brother. "That's why you're not eating any of it!"

Robert coughed, blushed, hunched his shoulders and muttered something in a language that didn't sound like English.

Dad coughed, blushed, hunched his shoulders and ransacked wardrobes in his mind, searching for words.

"Oh, it's er . . . fine, Alice! Fine!" he said. "Only . . . the marrow is just a little bit on the crunchy side."

"It's supposed to be *al dente*," sniffed Alice.

"And how about the stuffing?" Dad enquired. "Was that supposed to be crunchy too?"

"I wonder if I let the sausage meat defrost long enough?" Alice mused gloomily.

"Sausage meat?" spat Robert, throwing his knife and fork down with a disgusted clatter. "You mean you've actually given me food made out of some poor dead pig that's been hacked to pieces and ground down in a mincer? You know I'm trying to become a vegetarian!"

Alice's eyes twinkled with tears of outrage.

"Oh, yes?" she replied scathingly. "And what about that cheeseburger

6

you scoffed last week, Mr Ozone
Friendly?"

"That was different!" yelled Robert.
"I needed the protein! I forgot to pack
my multi-vitamin tablets!"

Joan who could see but not hear the

7

argument from behind her wall of
music, bawled out, "Two pin-falls, two
submissions, or a knock-out!"

"That's enough!" boomed Dad, in
his sudden-death voice. "Alice! Rob!
You're old enough to realise that
people aren't perfect. Just because Rob
had a lapse in being a vegetarian
doesn't make him into a criminal. And
Alice might not be the world's greatest

cook yet, but she's trying her best.
Now settle down, both of you."

"And the referee's decision is final!"
Joan whispered hoarsely.

Mum came back into the dining
room. She looked so puzzled that the
frownlines made her forehead resemble

a freshly-ploughed field.

"You all right?" asked Dad.

"Mum!" shrilled Alice. "Do you want me to call a doctor?"

"No," said Mum. "That was my mother on the phone."

"When is she arriving?" asked Dad, trying to sound cheerful about it.

"She's not," said Mum. "She says she fancies a change this year, so she's going on holiday with some friends from the Pensioners' Club."

"Where are they going to boogie-on down?" mocked Dad. "Sunny Whitby? Morecambe?"

"The south of France," said Mum.

"You know," laughed Dad, "I thought you just said your mother was going to the south of France!"

"I did," said Mum, and Dad stopped laughing.

10

"B-but . . ." spluttered Alice, "the south of France is all sun and sand and sparkling sea and Granny Crump is all . . ."

"Grey clouds and wet slate," said Mum. "I know. Weird, isn't it?"

"It's worse than weird," grumbled Robert. "It's a waste!"

Chapter 2

AND SO GRANNY Sheppard was invited
to stay. The children liked Granny
Sheppard. She looked like a proper
granny, with bubbly white hair and
spectacle-frames like exotic butterflies.
She smelled of lavender and read
books whose covers showed ladies with
long, blonde hair being hugged by
doctors or soldiers or sailors. Best of
all, Granny Sheppard doted on her
grandchildren; they could twist her
round their little fingers.

On the first morning of her stay,
Granny Sheppard was up long before

anyone else, pottering about in the kitchen. Mum and Dad came downstairs to find the dining table covered with a white lace cloth. There was a small bowl of flowers in the centre of the table.

"I've seen to breakfast," Granny said. "Bacon, eggs and fried bread for you, Geoffrey."

"But!" said Dad.

"You're going to work," Granny said, sweetly but firmly. "I know you, Geoffrey! You'll be stuffing yourself with chocolate bars at eleven o'clock if you don't have a proper breakfast." She turned to Mum. "And I know you don't like a fried breakfast, so I've made scrambled eggs on toast."

"But!" said Mum.

"Oh, and I hope you don't mind, Susan dear," Granny continued

13

sweetly and quickly, "only I didn't use that brown-bread-with-bits-in that I found in the bread bin. It gives me heart-burn. I brought some white, sliced bread with me, so I've made the toast with that. Now then," Granny smiled dazzlingly, "sit down and I'll serve up. Tea or coffee, dears?"

Mum and Dad sat, stunned.

"How does she manage it?" hissed Mum. "I haven't even worked out who I am yet, and she's cooked breakfast for six!"

Before Dad could reply, Robert and Alice appeared. They seemed less surprised by Granny Sheppard's ability to wake up in the morning. Joan rumbled down the stairs and burst into the dining room, clicking her fingers.

"Hi, Mum!" she cried. "Hi, Dad!

Hi, Bobby! Hi, Ally! Hi, Gran!" She glanced at the table, saw bacon and scrambled eggs and grimaced. "Mega-horrible!"

"Ah, I thought you might not like what the others are having, Joan dear," said Granny. "I remembered that when your father was your age, he went through a junk-food stage, so I've warmed up a tin of Space Devils for you."

"Space Devils!" Joan announced, in perfect imitation of the voice in the TV advertisement. "The pasta snack in a cheesy, curry sauce. Fill the space in your little devils."

"Very good," said Granny, sweetly and tactfully. "Just you sit down, dear, and Granny will get your breakfast directly."

"White, sliced toast," sighed Mum, gazing at the toast rack. "Probably full of chemicals and hormones. Our brown bread is totally organic."

"Great toast, Gran!" Robert called into the kitchen.

"Thank you, dear," replied Granny, with a beam in her voice.

"Better than the bread we normally have," said Alice. "It's brown with bits on it and the crusts go rock-hard when you toast it."

Granny Sheppard placed a steaming plate in front of Joan and then stood in the kitchen doorway with her arms folded and her mouth stretched in a smile like a ray of sunshine. It was a smile which quietly and radiantly defied anyone to complain about anything.

Granny Sheppard's smile warmed and ruled the house for two days, until it began to feel uncomfortable. Every ten minutes (or so it seemed), Granny would disappear into the kitchen and reappear with freshly-baked cakes and biscuits, or home-made lemonade, or a meal for the whole family.

Robert was too busy eating to play his electric guitar, Alice got back from a riding lesson to find a hot, bubbly bath waiting for her, Joan acquired a new set of headphones and Mum worried.

"I'm getting lazy!" she confided to Dad. "She's doing the washing, the ironing and the cooking. She's spoiling us as well as the kids."

"Don't worry!" smiled Dad. "She's enjoying herself. Anyway, in a few days she'll go home and then everything will get back to normal."

Mum had a nagging feeling at the

back of her neck, as though something were trying to tell her that Dad was wrong, but she shrugged and ignored it.

That very evening, disaster struck. The children were sprawled in front of the television, Mum and Dad were having a quiet glass of sherry in the dining room and Granny Sheppard was bustling about in the kitchen, smiling as she chopped and boiled and poached and grilled.

The front-door bell rang.

"I'll get it," said Dad.

"It's probably one of Rob's mates," said Mum. "He mentioned that someone might call."

But it wasn't one of Robert's mates. When Dad opened the front door, he was almost knocked over by a small avalanche of luggage. Behind the

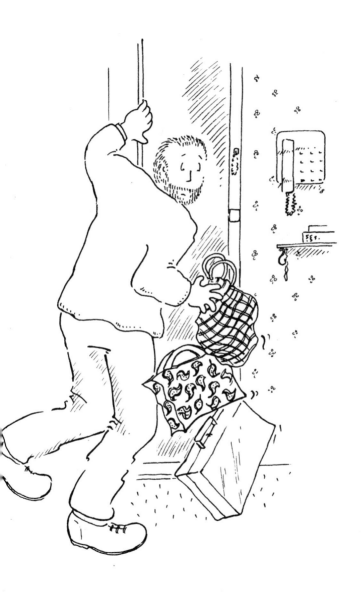

avalanche stood a tall, thin, elderly lady with a mouth that looked as though it had just finished sucking a lemon.

"Granny Crump!" yelled Dad.

"Aye," said Granny Crump. "You're right there, lad! Are you going to let me come in, or do you expect me to expire on the doorstep?"

"B—but . . . I thought you were in the south of France!" gabbled Dad.

"I was," said Granny Crump, stepping into the hall, "but I've come back early to stay with you. France was terrible! Hot sunshine all the time! Couldn't get a decent cup of tea anywhere! And the place was jam-packed with foreigners – they wouldn't speak English, no matter how loudly I shouted. The food gave me the steaming collywobbles, and as for the

toilets. . . !" Granny Crump groaned and rolled her eyes. "Just a hole in the floor with footpads and a grip for your teeth! I said to Mavis Bunridge – *Mavis* – I said – *if this is what they mean by exotic continental life, then I don't much like it . . .*"

Granny Crump continued for some time. The sound of her voice attracted Joan, Alice and Robert to the doorway of the front room. They stared at their grandmother with white, dismayed faces. Granny Crump's voice also drew an astonished Mum out of the dining room and, at long last, Granny Sheppard, who appeared with a welcoming smile and a cup of tea.

When Granny Crump caught sight of Granny Sheppard, she stopped her detailed account of the effects of French food on her digestive system.

Her mouth clamped shut with an audible snap.

"Oh!" she said curtly. "I see! So this is what goes on while I'm away, is it?"

The atmosphere at the dinner table was enough to give a polar bear the shivers. Granny Crump treated Granny Sheppard's presence as a personal insult and it made her sigh a lot. Granny Crump's sighs were long, juddering affairs that made the cutlery rattle.

Granny Sheppard tried her best to remain cheerful, but before long even her relentless smile had shrunk a few centimetres.

"Are you enjoying your Ghoulish Gobbets, Joan, dear?" she asked.

"They're mega-yummy, Gran!" rapped Joan.

"That child will come to no good, mark my words," Granny Crump intoned. "All that junk food will soften her brain. Plenty of cabbage, that's what she needs. Cabbage and swede!"

Alice remembered what Granny Crump's cabbage and swede tasted like and the blood drained from her face.

"I don't think I can eat any more," she whined.

"That's too much television for you," Granny Crump said confidently. "It's a well-known fact that television kills a child's appetite and stunts its growth."

"Well, I watch TV and I'm not stunted!" Robert guffawed.

Granny Crump fixed her grandson with a look that would have turned back a Great White Shark.

"But you don't get enough exercise!" she snapped. "That's why you've got all those spots. Exercise and opening-medicine, that's the ticket for you, my lad."

"But, Ada, dear," Granny Sheppard intervened, "children are rather different from what they were in our day."

"Aye, you're right there, Mary," agreed Granny Crump. "Nowadays

children have got soft brains, stunted growth and spots!"

Granny Sheppard's smile shone like the sun on a frozen pond.

After dinner, Mum and Dad tried reason, persuasion and bribery to get one of the grannies to go home, but neither would budge. Even the prospect of sharing a bedroom didn't put them off.

The Sheppard family sank into a deep gloom.

Chapter 3

THE NEXT MORNING, it became apparent that the swords the grannies had crossed during dinner had merely been preparation for a full-scale joust. The Sheppards woke early to the realisation that all was not well. From downstairs came ominous murmurings, sizzlings and bubblings and a mixture of smells that was faintly alarming.

When the family bumbled into the dining room, they were greeted by two eager-looking grannies.

"I've made tea and coffee," smiled Granny Sheppard.

"And I've made cocoa," said Granny Crump.

"And there's ham and eggs, and waffles and jam!" said Granny Sheppard, just a shade smugly.

"Yankee muck!" scowled Granny Crump. "Have a bowl of High Fibre Munchies."

The Sheppards glanced at each other helplessly. To choose anything would be to choose sides, which would mean offending one, or both grannies.

It was Joan who saved the situation by staying calm and thinking quickly. She did this quite often, but it was always at times when the rest of the family was panicking too much to notice. In the quiet voice that she saved for common-sense suggestions, she said, "The thing is, Grans, we all got a bit fat on holiday, so we've decided to go on a diet."

"Eh?" said the two grannies.

"So it's crisp-bread and mineral

water all round!" said Joan.

"Yeah! That's right," Robert agreed reluctantly.

Alice nodded; being deprived of waffles and jam temporarily robbed her of speech.

"Ee!" exclaimed Granny Crump, arms akimbo. "Well, I'll go to the foot of our stairs! I got up at five o'clock to start cooking."

"So did I!" whimpered Granny Sheppard, dabbing at the corners of her eyes with a lilac tissue. "One doesn't expect to be showered with gratitude, but a little consideration never goes amiss. You only needed to mention that you were dieting, Geoffrey."

"I'm starting to feel guilty!" Mum muttered to Dad.

"I'm starving!" muttered Dad. "Loads of great food on the table, and

34

all I can do is crunch a few
crisp-breads."

On his way home from work, Dad
stopped off to buy two large bunches of
flowers as a peace-offering for the
grannies. When he opened the front
door, he saw a large display of flowers

on the hall table. There were more flowers in the living room.

Mum was in the kitchen, slicing red peppers. She laughed when she saw the bouquet Dad was holding.

"You too, eh?" she said. "I went and bought some this morning and so did the kids. I think there are more flowers in the house than there are at the florist's!"

Dad looked gingerly around the kitchen.

"Where are the terrible twins?" he asked. "Don't tell me they've gone home?"

"No," said Mum, "they've gone out together. They spent all morning nattering and then they said they were going shopping. Your mum is taking my mum out for a meal, and my mum is taking your mum to see a film."

"A film?" frowned Dad. "Have you

seen the films that are on in town?"

"They both seemed keen on the idea," Mum shrugged.

By eleven-thirty, Mum was fidgeting with the arm of a chair and Dad was pacing up and down the living room.

"Shall I phone the police?" he fretted.

"Let's not get too worried yet," Mum advised.

"I'm already too worried," moaned Dad. "It's hysteria I'm trying to avoid!"

"The film only finished an hour ago," Mum said reassuringly.

"An hour?" gasped Dad. "What can two elderly women get up to round here for an hour at this time of night?"

A car drew up outside. Mum and Dad listened expectantly, but their faces fell when they heard the sound of loud voices and raucous, whooping laughter.

"Lager louts!" said Dad disapprovingly. "I hope the grannies don't run into that lot."

The voices got louder. The laughter drew nearer. Mum and Dad stared at one another in disbelief as the door bell rang.

"What on earth. . . ?" muttered Dad.

38

Then the letterbox rattled and the
voice of Granny Sheppard called,
"Geoffrey? Come on, do shake a leg!
Ada's dying to tiddle!"

More laughter followed.

"You don't think. . . ?" began
Mum.

"They can't be!" said Dad.

"It sounds as if they are!"

When Mum and Dad opened the
front door, they found Granny Crump

and Granny Sheppard leaning on one another, swaying slightly. Their faces were flushed and their eyes were bright.

"Mother, you're drunk!" exclaimed Dad.

"Relaxed, Geoffrey," Granny Sheppard corrected, sweetly and uncertainly. "Ada and I went to The Red Lion when the film finished. I've been drinking gin and tonic."

"And I've been drinking rum and blackcurrant!" added Granny Crump.

"Mum," said Mum sternly, "how many rums have you had?"

"We didn't count, did we Mary?" tittered Granny Crump.

"We *lost* count, Ada!" chuckled Granny Sheppard. She coughed, regained her composure and said, "Ada and I have decided we're not

appreciated here. We're leaving tomorrow morning for a little holiday in Bournemouth."

"Together?" chorused Mum and Dad.

"Aye!" beamed Granny Crump. "We're off to Bournemouth for fun and frolics! Now, Mary, if you wouldn't mind steering me towards the lav – my legs have got a mind of their own tonight!"

Mum and Dad watched open-mouthed as the four legs of the two grannies weaved their way upstairs.

"They've made friends!" said Mum. "After all these years."

"I wonder . . ." croaked Dad.

"What?"

"Maybe we should ring up and warn Bournemouth what to expect!"

said Dad. "I think when those two hit the town, there won't be a lot left afterwards!"

Pet Hates

Chapter 1

AS SOON AS the screaming started in the front room, Mum and Dad rushed through from the kitchen. They arrived at the front-door at the same time and Dad barked his shin against the door frame as they squeezed through.

Joan was in an armchair, sitting as still as a fridge. Her face was white and her eyes were unusually wide and solemn. Alice was hunched up on the sofa with her face in her hands and her shoulders pumping up and down as she sobbed.

"What is it?" panted Dad.

"What's wrong?" Mum demanded.

Alice raised her tragic, tear-stained face and tried to speak, but all that would come out was, "Look!"

Mum and Dad looked. Nothing was broken and there was no blood anywhere; in fact the front room looked perfectly normal. Mum knelt down in front of Alice and held her shoulders.

"Come on, love," she coaxed gently. "Try and tell us what's upsetting you."

"It's. . . !" whimpered Alice. "It's . . . it's . . ."

"Gulpula's snuffed it!" announced Joan.

Mum and Dad turned to look at the goldfish bowl on the table in the corner. A little orange shape floated forlornly on the surface of the water.

Dad went closer to investigate.

"Poor old goldfish!" he said. "Remember when I won him at that fairground?"

"*Her*, you mean," insisted Alice. "I always knew Gulpula was a girl. She was so graceful and feminine."

"Graceful?" repeated Dad. "She just sort of swam around, opening and closing her mouth."

"Well, I'm sure she's gone to a better place now," said Alice, brushing tears from her face.

For a second, Dad tried to imagine what Goldfish Heaven might be like, but he shook his head quickly to rid himself of the idea, then picked up the goldfish bowl and left the room.

"Try not to be too sad, Alice," said Mum. "Gulpula had a good, long life and she died peacefully."

"Yes," snivelled Alice. "You're right, I suppose."

"Mum, can I have the body?" asked Joan. "I could pour plastic stuff over it and make a pendant!"

"No!" cried Alice. "I'm going to bury her. There's a rose bush in the garden that I can see from my bedroom window. I'm going to wrap Gulpula up in one of my best lace handkerchiefs, put her in a tin and bury her under the rose bush. Then, every morning I can look out of the window and remember her."

"That's a lovely thought," said Mum.

"I think you're dead soppy!" Joan told her sister.

Alice took a deep breath, composed herself and stood up just as Dad reappeared, empty-handed.

47

"I'm going to bury Gulpula!" Alice declared bravely.

"Oh, no need to bother, love," said Dad. "I've just flushed her down the loo."

Alice hurled herself back on the sofa and howled into a cushion.

"What did I do?" mumbled Dad. "Someone tell me what I did!"

"I'll explain it all in the kitchen," said Mum.

She took Dad by the elbow and steered him out into the hall.

"Alice is at a very impressionable age," she said in a low voice.

Dad's eyebrows curved up into cathedral arches.

"If this is only an impression, what's the real thing going to be like?"

Alice came down for dinner with a

black shawl over her shoulders.

"Are you feeling better now?" Mum asked.

Alice nodded mutely and crossed the room as though heavy weights had been tied to her shoulders. When she saw her plate, her face went longer than a lift-shaft.

"Fish and chips?" she gasped. "How can you all sit there eating fish and chips after what's happened?"

"Don't worry, it's not goldfish!" chuckled Robert.

"Thar she blows! Ha-har!" squawked Joan, harpooning her fish finger with a fork.

"That's what I like about this family," commented Dad. "We all rally round sympathetically in times of crisis."

"Well, I'll tell you what I've been

51

thinking," Mum said tactfully. "Perhaps we should get another goldfish. It's good to have a pet around the place."

"Oh, not another goldfish!" moaned Alice. "Not after Gulpula. It just wouldn't be right."

"I agree," said Robert.

Dad looked at Robert sharply. When Robert and Alice agreed, it made imaginary alarm-bells ring in Dad's head.

"Me too," exclaimed Joan, nodding her head so fast that it made her look as though she had two faces. "Goldfish are boring!"

Dad looked at Mum wild-eyed and signalled her frantically to change the subject, but he was a fraction of a second too late.

"What sort of pet would you like,

then?" Mum asked innocently.

"An Irish wolfhound," said Robert. "I've always liked them. They're cool!"

"A pony!" said Alice. "We could convert the back garden into a paddock. I've always dreamed of having a pony."

"Don't wanna big dog!" howled Joan. "We'd have to take it for long walks all the time. Ponies are for girly-wirlies! We need a small pet that's cuddly, easy to take care of and cheap to feed."

Dad gazed at Joan in astonishment.

"I never thought I'd live to say this," he said, "but Joan's idea is very sensible. Something small and cuddly, easy to take care of and cheap to feed –"

"Like a tarantula! Yeah!" bawled

Joan. She turned her left hand into a
tarantula and stroked it with her right
hand while she made cooing noises.

"What about a German Shepherd?"
mused Robert.

"Do you mean a dog, or an actual
person?" Dad blurted in panic.

"A goat!" bubbled Alice. "Goats are
lovely."

"Don't talk mental!" spat Robert.

"I am not mental!"

"Pyth-o-o-o-ns!"yelled Joan,
banging her fork on her plate.

Mum rested her head wearily on
Dad's shoulder.

"What have I done?" she whispered.
"They'll be rowing for weeks."

"Don't crack up on me now, Sue,"
hissed Dad. "We can face it, as long as
we stand together."

Chapter 2

PET WARFARE RAGED among the Sheppard children for several days, until Mum and Dad totally banned further discussions on the subject; but Alice and Joan kept taking animal encyclopaedias out of the library and Dad suspected that Robert was secretly writing out long lists of the largest, most expensive dogs he could think of.

And then, one day, Dad noticed that peculiar things were happening. Joan was talking to Alice without her headphones on. All three children were holding conferences in Robert's bedroom, which was usually out-of-bounds-on-pain-of-death for the girls.

"I don't like it," Dad told Mum in the kitchen one evening. "They're up to something."

"Don't be so suspicious, Geoff!" said Mum. "They're just getting on with one another at the moment. Even the happiest families don't row all the time."

"We've had it!" croaked Dad. "I know we've had it. They're ganging up on us. Only the S A S can help now!"

Just then, Robert, Alice and Joan appeared in the kitchen doorway. There was much whispering, smirking and elbowing, and then Robert cleared his throat.

"Mum? Dad? We've made a

decision about the family pet. All three of us."

"Great Scott!" breathed Dad. "Well, are you going to let us know the worst? What is it? A giraffe . . . or a hyena, perhaps?"

"Joan," said Mum curiously, "are you wearing one of my bras again?"

"No."

"Only . . . your chest is sort of . . . moving about."

Joan's chest was doing more than moving about. Her jumper was wriggling and jerking and making high-pitched "meep" noises, and then all three Sheppard children started talking at once.

"A girl I know from school –"

"Really cute, Dad –"

"– giving them away –"

"Mega cheap to feed!"

A black kitten burst out of the neck of Joan's jumper and started to walk over her shoulders.

"Isn't it sweet!" cried Mum.

"It is a cat, isn't it?" snapped Dad. "I mean, it isn't a panther cub, or anything?"

"It's just an ordinary, street-wise moggie," said Robert.

"He's not ordinary," protested Alice. "He's the most beautiful and

wonderful kitten in the world!"

"He pooed in my bedroom and it smells super-disgusting!" beamed Joan.

"You like cats?" Dad asked Mum, out of the side of his mouth.

"Check," said Mum, out of the side of hers.

"Right!" said Dad briskly. "The Sheppard family are now officially cat-owners. Alice, I want full details of where the kitten came from later. Let's get this straight, kids, this cat is your idea, so he's your responsibility. You feed him and clear up his messes."

"No problem," nodded Robert.

"Agreed!" shuddered Alice.

"Crucial!" screeched Joan. "We need to buy a litter tray, feeding bowls, a flea collar – and we must have a pooper-scooper."

"And no feeding him from the table," Dad warned.

Robert, Alice and Joan made reluctant oh-all-right-then noises.

"Thank goodness that's settled at last," sighed Mum.

Much later, Dad tried to work out what came over him. Perhaps it was the strain, or perhaps he was light-headed with relief. Whatever the reason, he suddenly found himself saying, "What are you going to call him?"

"Simba," said Robert confidently. "That's a good, macho name."

"He's far too delicate for a name like that," countered Alice. "I think we should call him Jason, or Godfrey."

"I wanna call him Spike!" rumbled Joan.

"Spike?" jeered Robert. "Trust you to come up with a stupid name like that."

"It's not a stupid name, zit-face!"

Dad rested his head wearily on Mum's shoulder.

"Tell me I'm an idiot," he groaned.

"You're an idiot," said Mum. "You deal with Rob and Joan, I'll deal with

Alice. If we're lucky, it won't come to tears."

"If we're lucky, it won't come to blows!" Dad said miserably.

Age Concern

Chapter 1

IT WAS UNUSUAL for Dad to be last
downstairs in the morning, but nobody
noticed. Nobody noticed the brooding
look on his face, either. Robert was
face-down in a bowl of cornflakes,
looking as though he were in an eating
contest and well on the way to
winning. Alice was concentrating hard
on slicing her toast into exactly
equal-sized pieces. Joan was feeding
Claws, the black kitten, under the
table while she jiggled about to the
music of her personal stereo. Mum was
out in the kitchen, pouring herself a

cup of coffee, while she read the front page of the newspaper.

Dad slumped against the kitchen doorway.

"I took a look in the bathroom mirror, this morning," he said grimly. "A good, hard look. Under all the soap-splashes and greasy fingerprints, I saw my face."

"Coffee?" Mum asked absently.

"I've got wrinkles at the corners of my eyes," Dad complained. "There are white patches in my beard and if I bend my head right forward, I can see my bald spot."

"Toast?" enquired Mum.

"Just coffee!" Dad sighed. "I can't face the idea of eating anything this morning."

He took his coffee into the dining room and sat down heavily in a chair.

"Dad," said Robert, "I need some money for a school trip to the theatre next Wednesday evening. A fiver should do it."

"Next Wednesday?" grunted Dad.

"And don't forget the dance concert next Wednesday," Alice reminded her father. "You promised you'd come. I'm dancing the part of Queen of the Fawns."

"Wednesday!" Dad said softly. "Wednesday's child is full of woe . . . or is it Thursday's child?"

"Pretty!" exclaimed Joan. "Pretty kitty!"

"I wonder where all the years slip away to?" Dad whispered.

Then, at last, a member of the Sheppard household noticed Dad. The kitten leapt onto Dad's right leg, wrapped its paws around him and sank in its claws.

"Argh!" yelled Dad. "Get off, you great brute!"

"He loves you zillions!" crooned Joan. "Claws loves Dad to bits!"

"You shouldn't shout at cats," Alice remarked severely. "It gives them complexes."

"I've got complexes," muttered Dad.

"Er, if you're strapped for cash, Dad, I'll take a cheque," said Robert, trying to be helpful.

Dad shrugged but didn't say anything.

Robert carried his cereal bowl out into the kitchen.

"What's wrong with Dad, Mum?" he asked furtively. "He seems a bit . . ."

"What?"

"Well, not his usual self."

"Oh?" said Mum.

Alice came through into the kitchen with her plate.

"I think Dad's having a personality crisis, Mum," she announced. "He shouted at the kitten."

"Oh?" said Mum.

"I'm off to work now," Dad called from the dining room. "Busy day ahead, must make an early start. I've left your money on the table, Rob."

Mum, Robert and Alice listened for the sound of the front door closing and then looked at one another in a concerned way.

Joan appeared in the kitchen doorway. She looked concerned, too.

"Dad didn't pull my hair before he left," she proclaimed. "He always gives my hair a tug, for luck."

"Oh!" said Mum sharply.

"Mum!" cried Alice. "Are you having a heart-attack?"

"No," said Mum, "but I've just realised something."

She was staring at the calendar that was stuck to the front of the fridge with a magnet.

"It's your dad's birthday next Wednesday. He'll be forty."

A shocked chill settled over the kitchen.

"Oh, cripes!" groaned Robert.

"Just think," said Alice, "I'll be the daughter of a middle-aged parent!"

"Will Dad be a pensioner?" giggled Joan.

Chapter 2

BEFORE DAD CAME home from work that evening, Mum called the children into the front room for a conference. She seemed uncertain of how to start and spent what felt like a long time pacing up and down, circling her hands as though winding a ball of invisible string. The children watched patiently as she passed to and fro, moving their heads like a crowd at a particularly slow tennis match.

"The thing is . . ." Mum began. "What I wanted to explain was . . . You see, it's like this . . ."

71

"Has she been at the sherry?" Alice asked Robert in a low voice.

"I don't think so," Robert replied. "She's walking in a straight line."

"I hope she hurries up," whined Joan. "I'm faint from lack of grub!"

"It's about your father," Mum declared. "You see, when men reach a certain age, they start to go through changes."

"Changes?" frowned Robert.

"What sort of changes?" quailed Alice.

"My father was a werewolf!" snarled Joan.

"You may find your father turning a bit moody," Mum explained. "He might seem perfectly happy at one moment, and then the next he'll snap at you for no reason at all."

The Sheppard children exchanged

glances as Mum continued.

"And he may start talking a lot about how things used to be when he was young. It's going to be difficult, I know, but if we're patient, I'm sure we can all come to terms with it."

"But . . . Mum," Robert pointed out gently, "Dad's like that already. He always has been."

"True," Mum admitted. "But it would be nice if you could indulge him for a little while. Make him feel special. Nothing too obvious, mind, or he'll twig what's going on."

"Leave it to us, Mum," Robert grinned confidently. "We'll get the old chap sorted out!"

When Dad got home from work, he was attacked. The front door had hardly closed behind him before a

small but powerful assailant
head-butted him in the stomach and
gripped him so tightly around the
waist that the remaining air was driven
from his lungs with a sound like a
leather sofa being sat upon.

When the white dots stopped
dancing in front of Dad's eyes, he
looked down. He saw pink tortoises
cartwheeling across the back of a
yellow jumper.

"Joan?" he gasped.

"Daddy! You're my own Daddy!"
chuntered Joan. Her face came up to
look and her arms pressed tighter.
"You are my father! Yeah!"

"I'm glad all that's sorted out,
then," grimaced Dad. "I've worried
for years that you might have thought
I was an eccentric millionaire who'd
taken you in out of pity when you were

a baby. Now, if you could see your way
to letting me go, I've got one or two
important things I'd like to get on
with. Like breathing."

"Anything for you!" oozed Joan.

Dad freed himself from Joan's grip,
knowing how an ant feels when it
drags itself clear of a pool of golden
syrup. He did not get far down the
hallway, however, before he came face
to face with Alice, who was beaming
soupily.

"Why, Dad, it's you!" she gushed.

"Is it?" said Dad, glancing around
for an imposter. "So it is! And – just to
set the record straight – you're Alice,
and you're my daughter. If there's
anyone else who needs identifying,
would you kindly ask them to wait
until I've had a cup of tea? It's been a
hectic day and I'm –"

"You know," fluttered Alice, "I'm really, really glad I was born after Robert."

"Super!" said Dad. "Though perhaps it's just as well. There wasn't a lot of choice about it."

"I'm really, really glad I was the first little girl in your life!" Alice simpered.

"Alice," Dad shuddered, "have you been watching some new TV soap opera that I don't know about?"

"Soap operas?" Alice laughed dismissively. "Who needs soap operas with a wonderful family like ours? And it's all thanks to you, Dad."

She flitted across to her father and pecked him on the cheek.

Dad staggered into the dining room on his way to the kitchen, but he never made it. Robert stopped him by seizing his right hand. He squeezed Dad's hand until the bones crackled, then pumped it up and down vigorously, as though Dad were an engine that needed cranking.

"Hi, Dad! How was work?"

"Er . . ." squeaked Dad.

"Well, there you go!" cried Robert. "I know they're slave-drivers, but it's

partly your fault for being so good at
your job. You know, I was talking
about you today to Rick Spedding in
my class."

"You were?" said Dad.

Robert nodded.

"He said it must be great having a
father who's still young enough to
understand the feelings of someone my
age."

"That's smashing, Rob," croaked
Dad. "Now, if it's all the same to you,
I'd quite like to have my hand back. I
find it useful for doing things, like
making myself a cup of tea."

Robert let his father's hand go and
shouted out a laugh as he slapped
himself on the thigh.

"Brilliant crack, Dad! I must go and
tell the others!"

After Robert had gone, Dad rubbed

life back into his right hand and groaned.

"Darling?" Mum's voice came from the kitchen. "Is that you?"

"I don't really think so," Dad replied. "I think I must have changed into someone else while I was at work."

Chapter 3

DINNER WAS AN uneasy affair. Joan
made a tremendous fuss about sitting
next to Dad, and every so often she
would bump her head against his arm,
purring loudly in imitation of Claws.
Every time Dad caught sight of Alice,
she stretched her mouth into her
widest, most ghastly smile – the one
she used to charm presents out of
Granny Sheppard. It made a cold
sweat break out across Dad's temples.

Strangest of all, Robert stopped
eating before his lemon meringue pie
was completely finished, sat back in his

chair and said, "Hey, Dad, what sort of things did you use to do when you were my age?"

Dad blinked in bewilderment, like a small nocturnal mammal exposed to bright light.

"Er, well, Rob, of course we had to make our own amusements back in those days. I used to read comics and books, watch a bit of television, listen to pop music –"

"Check!" said Robert knowingly. "Frank Sinatra and Glenn Miller, right? Great stuff!"

"As it happens, Rob," Dad said slowly, "they were a bit before my time."

"I've seen some old photos of Dad," Alice stated. "He was a hippy!"

"What, with long hair?" gasped Robert.

"Oh, yes!" said Alice. "And bells and beads."

Joan narrowed her eyes wickedly.

"Did he wear flared trousers?"

"Yes!" snickered Alice. "Pink velvet ones!"

Joan did her hysterical breathing-in laugh that sounded like a klaxon announcing an emergency. Robert tried to turn a laugh into a cough and came up with a lough.

"And a big kipper tie with flowers all over it!" shrieked Alice.

Joan's laugh went up so high that a dog across the road started barking.

"And," Alice gurgled helplessly, "in one photo he's got his arm round this girl with long hair and a mini-skirt!"

"That's me," said Mum sadly.

She looked at Dad and they both

sighed in a depressed sort of way.

On the morning of his birthday, Dad
was the first one up. He made coffee
and fed Claws, whistling loudly and

cheerfully. One by one, the rest of the Sheppards appeared, mumbled sleepy happy birthdays and gave him cards and presents. Dad surveyed the little mound of gift-wrapped boxes on the dining table and rubbed his hands with glee.

"This is it, then!" he said eagerly. "The big four-oh! Life begins at forty, and I'm really looking forward to it. I've decided that looking back at the past is a waste of time! The thing to do is . . ."

His voice died away as he noticed the expressions on the faces of his family. They looked as though they were staring at something spectacularly grim and depressing.

"I'll be forty next year," droned Mum. "And I've started putting on weight again."

"I'll be thirteen this year," said Robert. "I woke up this morning and it sort of hit me all at once. I'm going to be a teenager!"

"I'll be ten in a couple of months!" sighed Alice. "My last year in Junior School. My last year in the enchanted garden of childhood!"

"I'm gonna be eight soon!" scowled Joan. "I don't wanna be eight! I used

to forget about eight when I counted
up to ten!"

The atmosphere in the dining room
was so dismal, that when Dad heard
the toaster twang, he was grateful to
have an excuse to go into the kitchen
and escape from it. While he was
buttering the toast, he felt the kitten
arch itself against him.

"Hello, puss!" Dad said. "You're

not worried about age, are you?"

The kitten wasn't worried about anything. In fact, it was so happy, it decided to leap up on Dad's left leg and sink its claws lovingly into his flesh.

"Argh!" yelled Dad. "If anyone in there wants to see me get to forty-one, grab a crowbar and get in here, quick!"

The resulting rush for the kitchen door made Dad feel quite flattered.